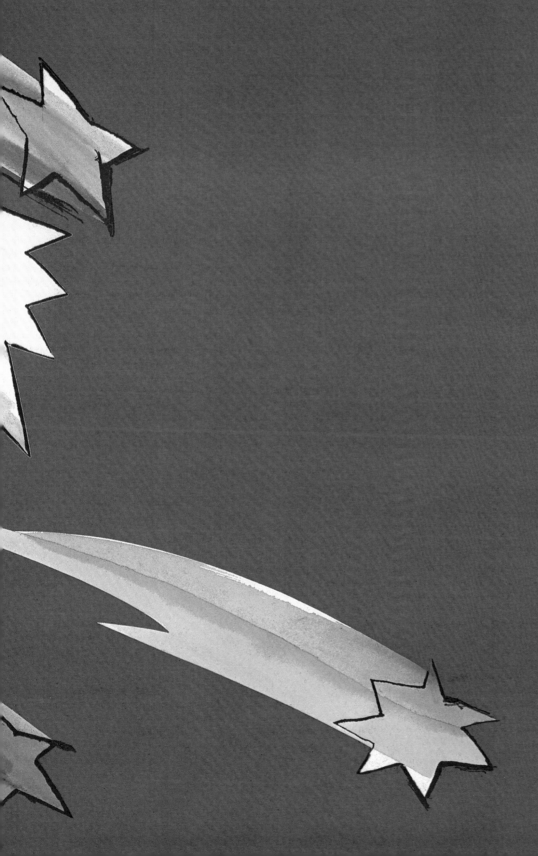

First published in 1984 by Andersen Press Ltd, London

Dual language edition published in 2012 by Mantra Lingua Ltd

Global House, 303 Ballards Lane, London, N12 8NP, UK

http://www.mantralingua.com

Copyright © 1984 Tony Ross

Dual language text copyright © 2012 Mantra Lingua Ltd

Audio copyright © 2012 Mantra Lingua Ltd

The rights of Tony Ross to be identified as the author and illustrator
of this work have been asserted by him in accordance with the
Copyright, Designs and Patents Act 1988

A CIP record of this book is available from the British Library

انا قادمٌ لأقبضَ عليكَ!

TONY ROSS

I'M COMING TO GET YOU!

Mantra Lingua

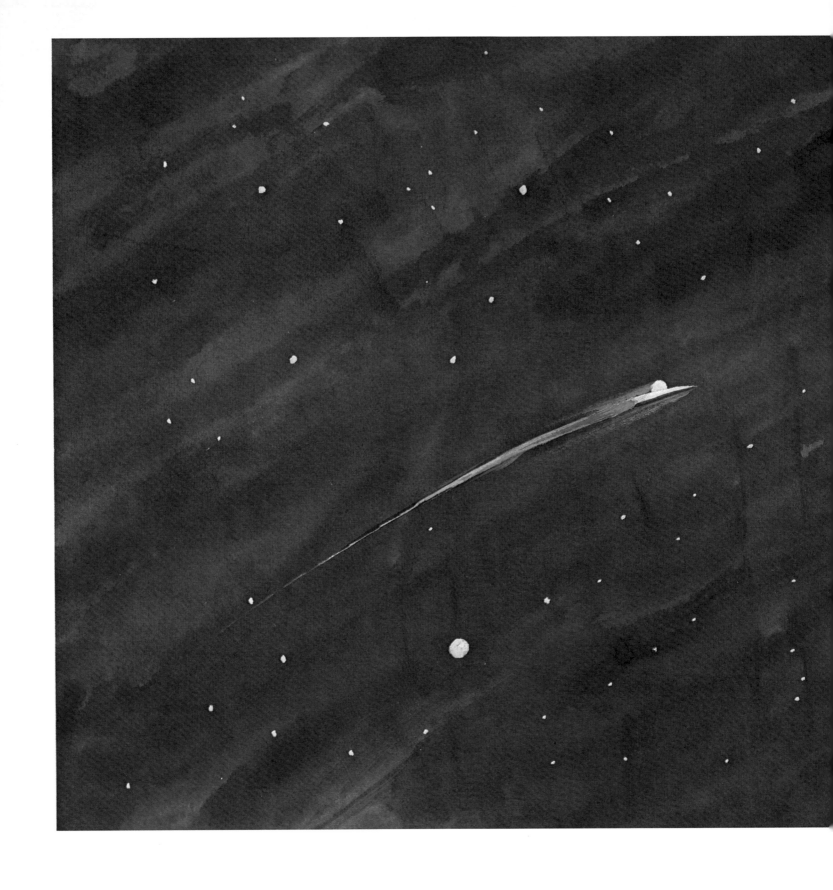

بعيداً عن مجرةٍ فضائيةٍ، كانت سفينةٌ فضائيةٌ تسرعُ

Deep in another galaxy, a spaceship rushed towards

نحوَ كوكبٍ صغيرٍ هادىء.

. . . a tiny, peaceful planet.

هبطتْ السفينةٌ فقفزَ منها وحشٌ كريه.

It landed, and out jumped a loathsome monster.

فصاحَ: "انا قادمٌ لأَقبضَ عليكَ!"

"I'm coming to get you!" it howled.

سحقَ الوحشُ شعبَ الموز اللطيفِ كله.

The monster crushed all the gentle banana people.

وحطّمَ تماثيلَهُم وبعثرَ كتبهم.

It smashed their statues, and scattered their books.

ومضغَ الجبالَ

It chewed up the mountains,

وشربَ المحيطات ثمّ تحلّى بقناديل البحر.

and drank the oceans. It had jellyfish for afters.

التهمَ الكوكبَ كلّه لكنّه لم يأكلْ...

It gobbled up the whole planet, except for . . .

قلبَه لأنه كانَ حاراً جداً ولا اطرافه لأنها كانتْ باردة جداً.

. . . the middle, which was too hot, and the ends,
which were too cold.

لكنّه لايزالُ جائعاً،

فطارَ في سفينتهِ الفضائيةِ يقضمُ النجومَ الصغيرةَ في طريقه.

Still hungry, the monster flew off in its spaceship,
nibbling small stars on the way.

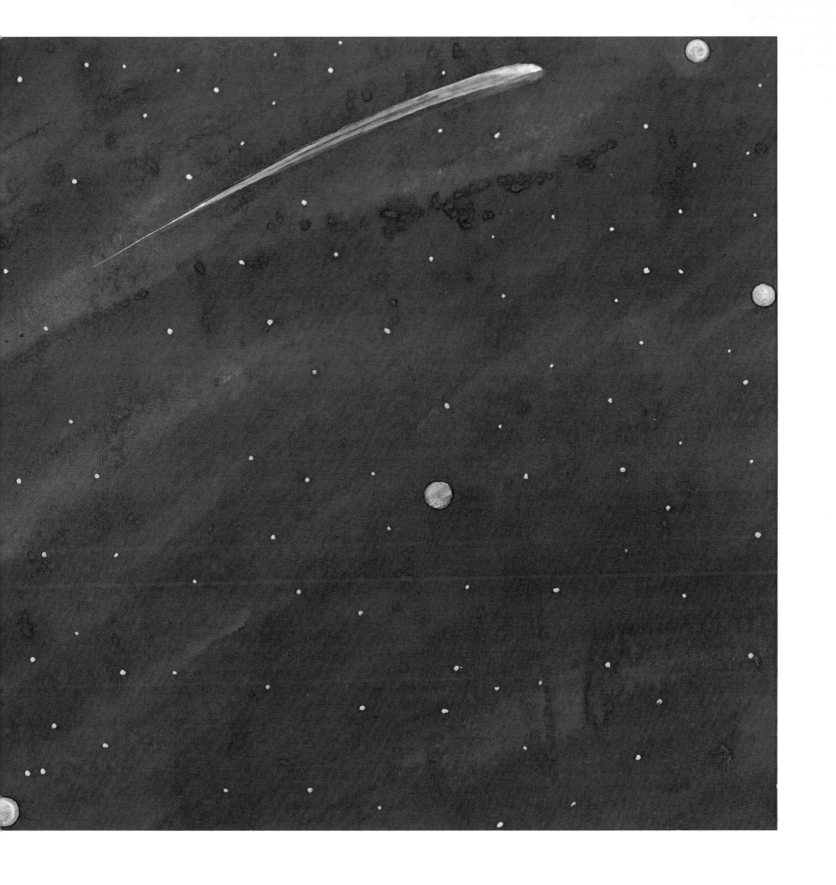

ثم رأى كوكباً جميلاً ازرقاً اسمُه الأرض.

It had seen a pretty blue planet called Earth.

فرأى على راداره صبيّاً اسمُه تومي براون.

فهدرَ: "انا قادم لأقبضَ عليكَ!"

The monster found little Tommy Brown on its radar.
"I'm coming to get you!" it roared.

كانَ قد حانَ وقتُ النومِ، وكانَ تومي يستمعُ الى قصةٍ عن
الوحوشِ المرعبة.

It was bedtime, and Tommy was listening to a story all about scary monsters.

اقتربتْ المركبةُ الفضائيةُ من الأرضِ، واكتشفَ الوحشُ اينَ يعيشُ تومي.

The spaceship neared Earth, and the monster found
out where Tommy lived.

دارَ في البلدةِ يفتِّشُ عن البيتِ المناسب.

It circled the town, looking for the right house.

بينما كانَ تومي صاعداً الى سريرهِ، كانَ يتفحّصُ كلَّ درجةٍ يفتشُ
عنِ الوحوش.

As Tommy crept up to bed, he checked every stair
for monsters.

كانَ يبحثُ في كل مكانٍ يمكنْ أن تختبىءَ فيه.

He looked in every place they could hide.

تخيّلَ أنهُ سمعَ صوتاً خافتاً من وراءِ النافذة.

Once, he thought he heard a bump outside his window.

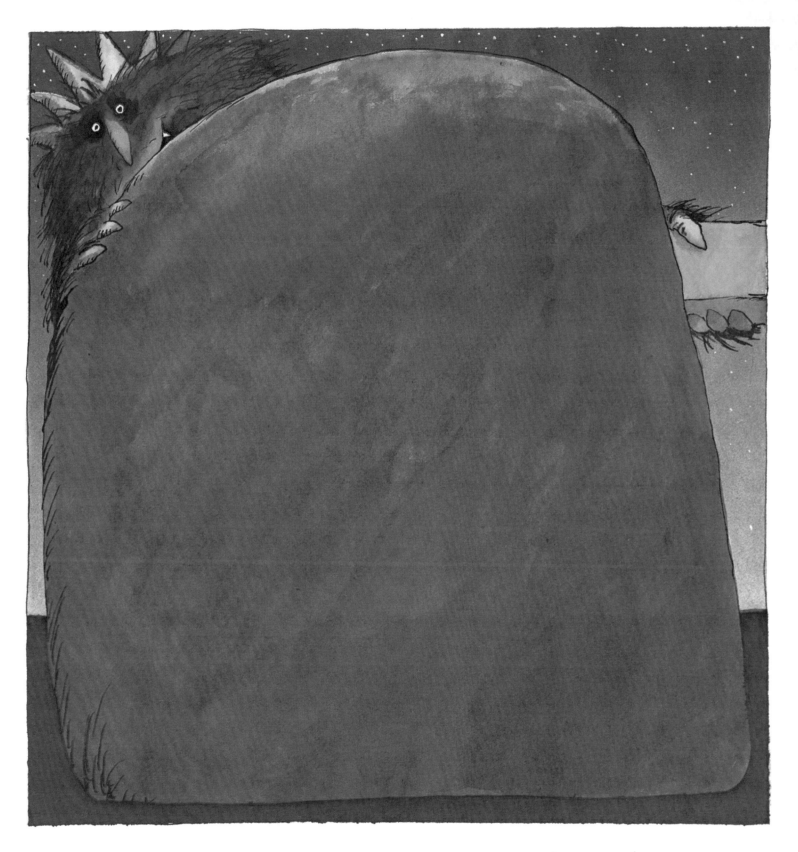

اختبأ الوحشُ وراءَ صخرةٍ وانتظرَ حتى الفجر.

"انا قادمٌ لأقبضَ عليكَ"، همسَ الوحش.

The monster hid behind a rock, and waited for the dawn.
"I'm coming to get you!" it hissed.

في الصباحِ ، نسِيَ تومي جميعَ الوحوشِ وذهبَ الى المدرسةِ فرحاً...

In the daylight, Tommy forgot all about monsters,
and he set off happily for school . . .

لكنْ حينذاكَ وبهديرٍ رهيبٍ انقضَ عليه الوحشُ!

. . . but then, with a terrible roar, the monster pounced!

Other Arabic and English books for 3-7 year olds

Aliens Love Underpants
Augustus and his Smile
Brrmm! Let's Go!
Dear Zoo
Farmer Duck
Fox Fables
Giant Turnip
Goal! Let's Play!
Goldilocks and the Three Bears
Goose Fables
Head, Shoulders, Knees and Toes
Keeping up with Cheetah
Lima's Red Hot Chilli
Lion Fables
Listen, Listen

Little Red Hen...Grains of Wheat
Nita Goes to Hospital
Row, Row, Row Your Boat
Sahir Goes to the Dentist
Sports Day in the Jungle
Three Billy Goats Gruff
Tom and Sofia Start School
Welcome to the World Baby
Wheels on the Bus
Wild Washerwomen
You're All My Favourites
Yum! Let's Eat!

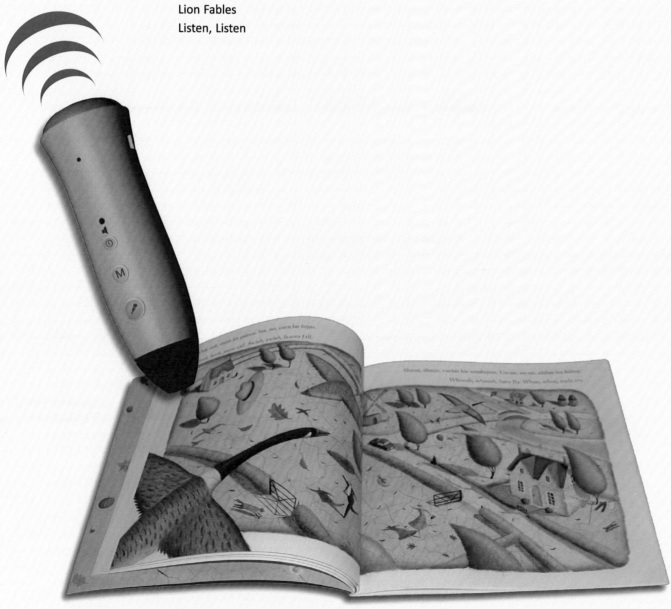